Curious George
Christmas Carols

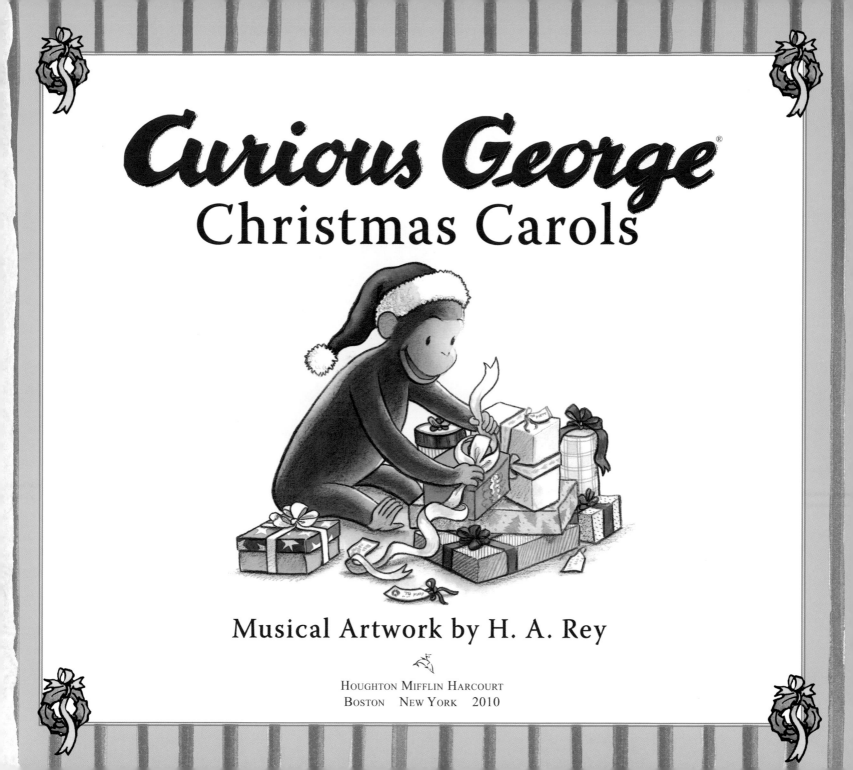

Musical Artwork by H. A. Rey

HOUGHTON MIFFLIN HARCOURT
BOSTON   NEW YORK   2010

CHRISTMAS TREE

O CHRISTMAS TREE, O Christmas tree,
how lovely are your branches.
In summer sun, in winter snow,
a dress of green you always show.
O Christmas tree, O Christmas tree,
how lovely are your branches.

O Christmas tree, O Christmas tree,
with happiness we greet you.
When decked with candles once a year,
you fill our hearts with Yuletide cheer.
O Christmas tree, O Christmas tree,
with happiness we greet you.

Come, All Ye Faithful

O COME, ALL YE FAITHFUL, joyful and triumphant,
O come ye, O come ye to Bethlehem.
Come and behold Him, born the King of angels.

O come let us adore Him,
O come let us adore Him,
O come let us adore Him,
Christ the Lord.

Sing, choirs of angels, sing in exultation,
Sing, all ye citizens of heav'n above.
Glory to God, glory in the highest.

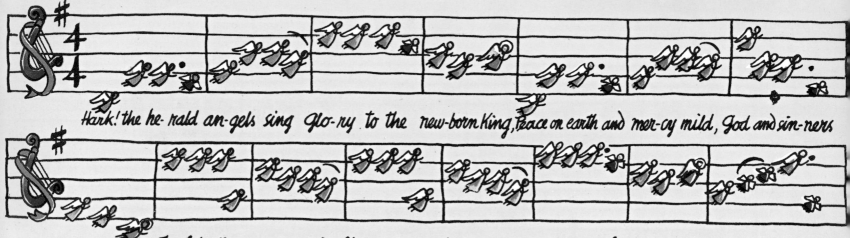

Hark! the he-rald an-gels sing Glo-ry to the new-born King, Peace on earth and mer-cy mild, God and sin-ners

re- con- ciled. Joy-ful all ye na-tions rise, Join the tri-umph of the skies With th'an-gel-ic host pro-claim Christ is born in

Beth-le-hem, Hark! the he-rald an-gels sing Glo-ry to the new-born King.

Hark! the Herald Angels Sing

Hark! the herald angels sing,
Glory to the newborn King.
Peace on earth and mercy mild,
God and sinners reconciled.
Joyful all ye nations rise,
Join the triumph of the skies.
With th' angelic host proclaim,
Christ is born in Bethlehem.
Hark! the herald angels sing,
Glory to the newborn King.

Hail the heaven-born Prince of Peace!
Hail the Son of Righteousness!
Light and life to all he brings,
Risen with healing in his wings;
Mild, he lays his glory by,
Born that man no more may die,
Born to raise the sons of earth,
Born to give them second birth:
Hark! the herald angels sing
Glory to the newborn King.

WE THREE KINGS

WE THREE KINGS of Orient are;
Bearing gifts we traverse afar,
Field and fountain, moor and mountain,
Following yonder star.

Star of wonder, star of night,
Star of royal beauty bright,
Westward leading, still proceeding,
Guide us to the perfect light.

Born a King on Bethlehem's plain.
Gold I bring to crown Him again.
King forever, ceasing never,
Over us all to reign.

Glorious now, behold Him arise,
King and God and Sacrifice.
Alleluia, alleluia,
Earth to the heav'ns replies.

I SAW THREE SHIPS

I SAW THREE SHIPS come sailing in,
on Christmas Day, on Christmas Day.
I saw three ships come sailing in,
on Christmas Day in the morning.

And what was in those ships all three,
on Christmas Day, on Christmas Day?
And what was in those ships all three,
on Christmas Day in the morning?

The Mother Fair and Christ were there,
on Christmas Day, on Christmas Day;
The Mother Fair and Christ were there,
on Christmas Day in the morning.

Pray, whither sailed those ships all three,
on Christmas Day, on Christmas Day?
Pray, whither sailed those ships all three,
on Christmas Day in the morning?

O they sailed into Bethlehem,
on Christmas Day, on Christmas Day,
O they sailed into Bethlehem,
on Christmas Day in the morning.

And all the bells on Earth shall ring,
on Christmas Day, on Christmas Day;
And all the bells on Earth shall ring,
on Christmas Day in the morning.

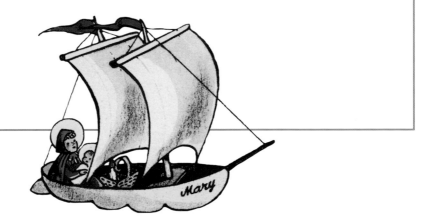

DECK THE HALL

Deck the hall with boughs of hol-ly,
Tis the sea-son to be jol-ly,
Fa-la-la-la-la, la-la-la-la. Don we now our

gay ap-par-el, Fa-la-la-la-la-la,-la-la-la. Troll the an-cient Yule-tide car-ol,

Fa-la-la-la-la, la-la-la-la.

DECK THE HALL

DECK THE HALL with boughs of holly.
Fa-la-la-la-la, la-la-la-la.
'Tis the season to be jolly.
Fa-la-la-la-la, la-la-la-la.
Don we now our gay apparel.
Fa-la-la-la-la-la, la-la-la.
Troll the ancient Yuletide carol.
Fa-la-la-la-la, la-la-la-la.
See the blazing Yule before us.
Fa-la-la-la-la, la-la-la-la.
Strike the harp and join the chorus.
Fa-la-la-la-la, la-la-la-la.
Follow me in merry measure

Fa-la-la-la-la-la, la-la-la.
While I tell of Yuletide treasure.
Fa-la-la-la-la, la-la-la-la.
Fast away the old year passes.
Fa-la-la-la-la, la-la-la-la.
Hail the new, ye lads and lasses.
Fa-la-la-la-la, la-la-la-la.
Sing we joyous, all together,
Fa-la-la-la-la-la, la-la-la.
Heedless of the wind and weather.
Fa-la-la-la-la, la-la-la-la.

LITTLE TOWN OF BETHLEHEM

O LITTLE TOWN of Bethlehem,
How still we see thee lie.
Above thy deep and dreamless sleep
The silent stars go by.
Yet in thy dark streets shineth
The everlasting light.
The hopes and fears of all the years
Are met in thee tonight.

For Christ is born of Mary,
And gathered all above,
While mortals sleep, the angels keep
Their watch of wond'ring love.
O morning stars, together
Proclaim the Holy birth!
And praises sing to God the King,
And peace to all on earth.

THE FIRST NOEL

THE FIRST NOEL the angel did say
Was to certain poor shepherds in fields as they lay.
In fields as they lay keeping their sheep
On a cold winter's night that was so deep.

Noel, Noel, Noel, Noel,
Born is the King of Israel.

They looked up and saw a star
Shining in the east, beyond them far.
And to the earth it gave great light,
And so it continued both day and night.

This star drew nigh to the northwest.
And over Bethlehem it took its rest.
And there it did both stop and stay,
Right over the place where Jesus lay.

Si - lent night, Ho - ly night. All is calm, all is bright. Round you Vir - gin

Moth-er and Child, Ho-ly In-fant so ten-der and mild. Sleep in heav-en-ly peace,

Sleep in heav-en-ly peace.

SILENT NIGHT

SILENT NIGHT, holy night.
All is calm, all is bright.
Round yon Virgin Mother and Child,
Holy Infant so tender and mild.
Sleep in heavenly peace,
Sleep in heavenly peace.

Silent night, holy night.
Shepherds quake at the sight.
Glories stream from heaven afar.
Heav'nly hosts sing Alleluia.
Christ the Savior is born!
Christ the Savior is born.

Silent night, holy night.
Son of God, love's pure light.
Radiant beams from Thy holy face,
With the dawn of redeeming grace.
Jesus, Lord, at Thy birth,
Jesus, Lord, at Thy birth.

GOOD KING WENCESLAS

GOOD KING WENCESLAS looked out,
on the Feast of Stephen,
When the snow lay round about,
deep and crisp and even;
Brightly shone the moon that night,
tho' the frost was cruel,
When a poor man came in sight,
gath'ring winter fuel.

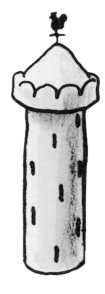

"Bring me flesh, and bring me wine,
bring me pine logs hither:
Thou and I will see him dine,
when we bring them thither."
Page and monarch, forth they went,
forth they went together;
Through the rude wind's wild
lament and the bitter weather.

JOYCE RASKIN, CHICK GRANING, AND JOE PROPATIER play in a rock band called SCARCE. They have toured throughout the United States, Canada, the United Kingdom, and Europe. This is their second CD for children. Ms. Raskin says this of their original music: "Our band has reinterpreted H. A. Rey's traditional Christmas Carols as a folksy, lighthearted, and kid-friendly set of recordings—a little Carter family, Mazzy Star, and Buddy Holly mixed together. We hope it's musical fun for kids of all ages."

The music notes in the illustrations of this book, arranged by Henry F. Waldstein, follow the more traditional melodies of these holiday songs that children and adults may already know. But as will be apparent to the listeners of our CD, there is plenty of room for reinterpretation of these favorite carols.

MUSICAL ART © COPYRIGHT 1944 BY H. A. REY, ARRANGED BY HENRY F. WALDSTEIN
CURIOUS GEORGE CHRISTMAS CAROLS COPYRIGHT © 2010 BY HOUGHTON MIFFLIN HARCOURT PUBLISHING COMPANY. All rights reserved.
Curious George illustrations by Greg Paprocki and Mary O'Keefe Young • Package design by Joyce White
ISBN 978-0-547-40861-3
Printed and manufactured in China   LEO 10 9 8 7 6 5 4 3 2 1
4500220053
HOUGHTON MIFFLIN HARCOURT PUBLISHING COMPANY • 222 BERKELEY STREET • BOSTON, MASSACHUSETTS 02116
WWW.HMHBOOKS.COM

Curious George